YOU MAY HAVE HEARD THE STORY of how a certain red-nosed reindeer was chosen to guide Santa's sleigh one foggy Christmas Eve. You've probably heard of the eight other reindeer, too. Maybe you can even remember all their names.

But you might be surprised to hear that there was a time, long ago, when Santa's sleigh was pulled not by a team of reindeer but by a single horse, named Silverbell.

In those days, Santa didn't have quite as many toys to deliver as he does now. But over the years, as more and more children believed in the magic of Christmas, Santa's list grew longer and longer. And his sleigh grew heavier and heavier. Santa knew that pretty soon, dear old Silverbell was going to need some help.

This is the story of how an ordinary family of reindeer became the most famous animals in the world. And it never would have happened if it weren't for a brave young doe named Dasher.

For Luke and Levi

Special thanks to Willow and Holly, the reindeer at the Stone Zoo in Stoneham, Massachusetts; Dave Banks; Benjamin and Everett Copleman; Rosemary Stimola; Katie Cunningham; Maryellen Hanley; and everyone at Candlewick Press who helped bring this book to life.

DASHER

MATT TAVARES

Walker Books
AND SUBSIDIARIES

LONDON · BOSTON · SYDNEY · AUCKLAND

LIFE WAS NOT EASY for the reindeer family
of J.P. Finnegan's Travelling Circus and Menagerie.
They spent long days crammed together under
the hot sun as an endless stream of curious people
jostled to catch a glimpse of them.

Even at night, there was little rest. Some nights, to pass the time, Mama would tell stories.

"It was a magical place," she would say. "The air was crisp and cold, and the ground was always covered with a cool blanket of white snow. Your father and I were free to roam under the glow of the North Star."

"Hello there," said the man. Dasher walked closer. The man smiled. "Have you ever pulled a sleigh?" he asked.

Dasher shook her head. "I've never even seen a sleigh," she said. "But I pull a wagon just about every night."

"Well," said the man, "how would you like to make a whole bunch of children really happy on Christmas morning?"

"I would like that very much," said Dasher.

Santa thanked Dasher and attached her harness. It was soft against her fur,
and its jingling bells made the most beautiful sound she had ever heard.

Santa climbed into his sleigh. Dasher pulled with all her might.

Then, suddenly, the load felt lighter. Dasher looked down...

They were flying!

All night, Dasher and Silverbell pulled Santa's sleigh through the air as Santa guided it from rooftop to rooftop, delivering toys to children everywhere. Dasher had never experienced such a thrill. And she ate so many carrots, she felt like she would burst!

She was having so much fun, she forgot all about the North Star.

As the first light of dawn appeared on the horizon,
they landed. The air was crisp and cold. The ground
was covered with a cool blanket of white snow.

Dasher searched for the North Star on the horizon,
but couldn't find it anywhere.

Santa smiled. "Dasher," he said. "Look up."

And there it was, directly overhead. "Is that …
the North Star?" she asked.

Santa's eyes twinkled. "Merry Christmas," he said.
"And welcome home."

The North Pole was just as wonderful as Mama's stories. Dasher roamed wherever she pleased, and Santa gave her all the carrots she wanted. But something was missing.

"I love it here," she told Santa. "But I miss my family. I wish we could be together."

Santa smiled. "That's your best wish yet, Dasher," he said. "Let's go and find them."

Late that night, Dasher guided Santa's sleigh all the way to J.P. Finnegan's Travelling Circus and Menagerie.

"Mama! Papa!" Dasher whispered. "Everyone, wake up!"

Mama lifted her head. "Dasher?" she said. "Is it really you?"

"It's me, Mama," said Dasher.

She told her family all about Santa, and Silverbell, and how the North Pole was just as amazing as Mama's stories.

"But I missed you," she said. "You were all I wished for."

Dasher led her family to Santa's sleigh, and Santa attached their harnesses.

"You're not going to believe this part," she said.

✳

When Christmas Eve arrived, Silverbell watched as Santa prepared his team.

"Are you sure you don't want to come?" asked Dasher.

"I'm sure," said Silverbell. "I know the eight of you will do a fine job."

Late that night, as Santa and his new team of reindeer soared around
the world, he called them by name for the very first time.

"Now, Dasher! Now, Dancer! Now, Prancer and Vixen! On, Comet!
On, Cupid! On, Donner and Blitzen!"

On Christmas morning, after all the toys had been delivered, they flew back to the North Pole, where they still live happily today.

There, the air is crisp and cold. The ground is always covered with a cool blanket of white snow.

And Dasher has everything she ever wished for.